Christmas Carol High School

by Mark Landon Smith

Baker's Plays
7611 Sunset Blvd.
Los Angeles, CA 90042
bakersplays.com

CHRISTMAS CAROL HIGH SCHOOL was first produced by Arts Live Theatre in Fayetteville, Arkansas from December 12-14, 2008. The performance was directed by Morgan Hicks, with costumes by Faye Alter, lighting and technical design by Mark Andrews, backstage crew was Morgan Vesper. The production stage manager was Karina Hunt. The cast was as follows:

MEREDITH . . . . .Emily Tomlinson

MONTY . . . . Baker Cinq-Mars

MELVIN . . . . Zach Stolz

TIFFANY . . . . Maryclaire Allen

BILLY . . . . Austin Ross

MELISSA . . . . Kaitlin Vesper

SERENA . . . . Huntley Hudgins

LYDIA . . . . Carley Tisdale

MS. CHENAULT . . . . Jules Taylor

GWENDOLYN . . . . .Sarah Howell

LILLIPUT . . . . Sarah Hierholzer

PATTY . . . . Ariana Franks

PATRICK . . . . .Cody Nielsen

ROGER . . . . .Ben Kieklak

LITTLE MEREDITH . . . . .Hadley Biggs

LITTLE MELISSA . . . . Milly Rogers

JOHN DAVID . . . . Coleman Snodgrass

VIOLET . . . . .Helen Maynard

JEREMY . . . . Jackson Heck

BRUNO . . . . Justin McClure

JULIE . . . . .Levi Gladd

ACE . . . . Brianna Folkes

SARAH . . . . Maddie Ritter

ISAAC . . . . Max Jardon

MICHAEL . . . . Sam Kieklak

STEPHANIE . . . . Samantha Soard

ELIZABETH . . . . Dianna Blaylock

CHARACTERS

The Students of West End High School:
(Total: 3m, 5f)

BILLY DARLING – Who plays the role of Capulet in "Romeo and Juliet"

MONTY FOLEY – Who plays the role of Second Capulet in "Romeo and Juliet"

MELVIN JEWSBURY – Who plays the role of Romeo in "Romeo and Juliet"

LYDIA IVEY – A cheerleader who also plays the role of Servant in "Romeo and Juliet"

MELISSA BARCLAY – A cheerleader and Meredith's "best friend" and the stage manager for "Romeo and Juliet"

MEREDITH PRIESTLY – Cheerleader Captain and Juliet in "Romeo and Juliet" and the meanest, nastiest girl in school.

TIFFANY BAINBRIDGE – A cheerleader

SERENA FAIN – A cheerleader

The Ghosts:
(Total: 3f or 2f, 1m)

GWENDOLYN CHESWICK – A confused Victorian ghost who comes to warn Meredith.

LILLIPUT – The Sprite of Christmas Present

DEATH – The ghost of Death. (may be double cast)

The Elementary Students from the Past:
(Total: 3m, 2f)

BRUNO – One of three tough kids who gang up on Little Meredith.

ACE – Another of the "tough gang."

ROGER – Another of the "tough gang."

LITTLE MEREDITH – An elementary school age version of Meredith.

LITTLE MELISSA – An elementary school age version of Melissa.

The Ghosts of Christmas Past Cheerleaders:
(Total: 1m, 1f)

PATTY PRINCE – A ghost and a 1950's cheerleader.

PATRICK PRINCE – Also a ghost, Patty's brother and a 1950's cheerleader.

The Present Elementary School Children:
(Total: 3m, 4f)

ISSAC
VIOLET
STEPHANIE
JOHN DAVID
SARAH
MICHAEL
JULIE

The Adults:
(Total: 2f)

MS. DELIA CHENAULT – West End High School's dramatic drama teacher
ELIZABETH BARCLAY – Melissa's older sister who is ill

Others:
(Total: 1f)

BEGGAR WOMAN – (may be double cast)

AUTHOR'S NOTE

Please see the APPENDIX section of the script there is a alternate scene written for the middle of scene five, in the event producers wish to omit the roles for small children.

SCENE BREAKDOWN

Scene One:
> The school stage of West End High School

Scene Two:
> Cheerleading practice, West End High School

Scene Three:
> Meredith Priestly's Bedroom

Scene Four:
> Meredith Priestley's Bedroom
> Elementary school playground
> West End High School Gymnasium

Scene Five:
> Meredith Priestly's Bedroom
> West End High School Gymnasium
> Melissa's Trailer
> Graveyard
> Street
> Meredith Priestly's bedroom

Scene Six:
> The school stage of West End High School

For Mom and Dad...

Scene One
Stage of West End High School

*(As the lights rise traditional pre-show Christmas music segues into Medieval music. The stage is bare, save for a few set pieces placed in front of the unit set which suggest a Medieval setting. We hear festive ad libs off-stage as a group of actors enter stage right dressed in Shakespearean garb. **BILLY DARLING**, who is playing the role of Capulet in the West End High School's production of "Romeo and Juliet," enters from stage left meeting the guests.)*

BILLY (AS CAPULET). Welcome gentlemen! Ladies that have their toes unplagued with corns will have a bout with you. Ah-ha! My mistress! Which of you all will now deny to dance? Come musicians, play! Give room and foot it, girls!

(The music plays as the guests begin to dance, all of whom are coupled except one gentleman who dances by himself, but dances as though he had a partner…)

More light, you knaves and quench the fire, the room is grown too hot.

*(The guests continue to dance as **BILLY** as Capulet addresses **MONTY FOLEY**, who is playing Second Capulet.)*

Ah, sirrah, this unlookt-for sport comes well.

Nay, sit, nay, sit, good cousin Capulet;

For you and I are past our dancing days:

How long is't now since last yourself and I were in a mask?

MONTY (AS SECOND CAPULET). By'r lady, thirty years.

*(As the dialogue continues, **MELVIN JEWSBURY**, as Romeo, enters from stage left. He is awkward and self-conscious; someone whom might best be describe as a nerd. He pretends to "hide" behind a set piece, which he, of course, knocks over, so as not to be noticed scanning the room.)*

BILLY (AS CAPULET). What, man! 'tis not so much, 'tis not so much:

'Tis since the nuptial of Lucentio,

Come Pentecost as quick as it will,

Some five-and-twenty years; and then we maskt.

MONTY (AS SECOND CAPULET). 'Tis more, 'tis more: his son is elder, sir;

His son is thirty.

*(**MELVIN**, as directed, "notices" someone from across the room…)*

BILLY (AS CAPULET). Will you tell me that? His son was but a ward two years ago.

*(**LYDIA IVEY**, playing the role of the servant, enters stage left bearing a large tray over laden with food, and begins to cross. **MELVIN**, as Romeo, stops her…)*

MELVIN (AS ROMEO). *(to **LYDIA** as the servant)* What lady's that, which doth enrich the hand of yonder knight?

LYDIA (AS SERVANT). I know not, sir.

MELVIN (AS ROMEO). O, she doth teach the torches to burn bright! Her beauty hangs upon the cheeks of night…

*(And from the back of the theatre we hear the thundering voice of **MS. DELIA CHENAULT**, the drama teacher, interrupting…)*

MS. DELIA CHENAULT. HOLD IT!

*(The music immediately stops as the dancers onstage instantly stop dancing, and turn to look out at the voice in the dark. At the same time the stage lights go down and the work lights come up. Not hearing, **MELVIN**, as Romeo, continues…)*

MELVIN (AS ROMEO). Like a rich jewel in a Ethiop's ear;…

MS. DELIA CHENAULT. *(as she is coming down the aisle)* HOLD IT! STOP!

MELVIN (AS ROMEO). *(still oblivious…)* Beauty too rich for use, for earth too dear!

LYDIA. *(to **MELVIN**)* Melvin, shut up! Ms. Chenault said stop!

MELVIN. *(to **LYDIA**)* Did I do something wrong?

(to himself)

I hope I didn't do something wrong!

*(to **MS. CHENAULT**)*

I'm sorry if I did something wrong.

MS. CHENAULT. *(from the foot of the stage)* No, Melvin, you did not do anything wrong. That was very nice. Thank you.

MELVIN. *(back to **LYDIA**)* That's a relief. I usually do something wrong.

MS. CHENAULT. Not this time.

(beat, then shouting for someone offstage)

MELISSA!

*(**MELISSA BARCLAY**, the production stage manager who is dressed completely in black, wearing a headset and carrying a script, enters from stage right…)*

MELISSA. Yes, ma'am?

MS. CHENAULT. Where, pray tell, is Meredith?

MELISSA. I don't know, ma'am. She was just here a….

MS. CHENAULT. *(overlapping **MELISSA**)* MEREDITH!

MELISSA. …moment a go.

MS. CHENAULT. MEREDITH PREISTLY!

MELISSA. *(joining in…)* MEREDITH!

MS. CHENAULT. *(wearily to **MELISSA**)* Find her.

MELISSA. Yes, ma'am.

(She turns to exit stage right and as she does continues to shout…)

MEREDITH! MEREDITH!

(**MS. CHENAULT**, *who is apparently fighting to maintain her mounting frustration, turns her back to the cast…waiting…*)

MELVIN. (*to* **MS. CHENAULT**) I'm glad it wasn't me who didn't do anything wrong.

MS. CHENAULT. Melvin…please…

(**MEREDITH PREISTLY**, *followed by* **MELISSA**, *enters in a bit of a huff with mussed hair and carrying a curling iron…*)

MEREDITH. (*to* **MELISSA**) Stop pushing! What's the rush?

(**MEREDITH** *then notices* **MS. CHENAULT**, *but is far from intimidated.* **MS. CHENAULT**, *on the edge of outrage, chooses her words carefully and methodically…*)

MS. CHENAULT. The "rush," Miss Priestly, is that you missed your cue, yet again, for which you had better have an excellent excuse.

MEREDITH. Of course I have an excellent excuse. I was crimping my hair. Duh.

MS. CHENAULT. Miss Priestly, "crimping your hair, duh" is *not* an excellent excuse. I requested each actor to come to the theatre with their hair already done.

MEREDITH. I didn't have time. Duh.

MS. CHENAULT. "Didn't have time…?"

MEREDITH. That's what I said. Right after school I had cheerleading championship practice, then I had to drop off my BMW to be detailed; get a quick mani and pedi – by that time I was *starving* so I swung by and picked up some sushi and came here. So you see, Ms. Chenault, quite obviously I didn't have time to do anything with my hair.

MS. CHENAULT. Everyone else in the cast *makes* the time. Why aren't you able to?

MEREDITH. Because *I*, unlike everyone else in this cast – have a life.

(*There is a tense pause…*)

MS. CHENAULT. Let us continue, please.

(as she starts back up the aisle)

Melissa, we will pick up with Romeo's line, "If I profane with my unworthiest hand."

MELISSA. *(to* **MS. CHENAULT***)* Yes, ma'am.

(to the cast)

PLACES!

(The cast assume their previous places as **MEREDITH** *crosses to her place beside* **MELVIN***)*

MS. CHENAULT. *(from whatever point in the house she has traveled)* LIGHTS!

(Instantly the work lights change to stage lights and the music begins to play. The actors begin to dance once again as before, except for **MEREDITH** *and* **MELVIN.***)*

MELVIN (AS ROMEO). If I profane with my unworthiest hand this holy shrine, then gentle fine is this, –
My lips, two blushing pilgrims, ready stand to smooth that rough touch with a tender kiss.

(There is a pause…)

MELISSA. *(poking her head onstage)* Meredith, it's your line.

MEREDITH. What?

MELISSA. It's your line!

MEREDITH. Oh.

(beat)

LINE!

MELISSA. "Good pilgrim, you do wrong your hand too much."

MEREDITH (AS JULIET). *(and she truly is a deplorable actress)* Good pilgrim, you do wrong your hand too much.

(There is a pause…)

LINE!

MELISSA. "Which mannerly devotion shows in this."

MEREDITH. Which mannerly devotion shows in this.

(There is a pause…)

LINE!

MELISSA. "For saints have hands that pilgrims' hand do touch,

And palm to palm is holy palmers' kiss.

MEREDITH. For saints have hands, blah, blah, blah…

MS. CHENAULT. *(from the house)* HOLD IT!

*(**MELISSA** re-enters.)*

MELVIN. Did I do something wrong?

*(Once again the music stops, the stage lights change to work lights and the dancers stop dancing, etc., as **MS. CHENAULT** starts walking up the aisle.)*

MEREDITH. *(out to the house in the direction of* **MS. CHENAULT***)* I don't have to kiss him, do I? He's got zits.

MELVIN. Just one.

MS. CHENAULT. *(as she walks up onto the stage)* Miss Priestly, I have studied Shakespeare for many, many, many, many years. And in that time I have *never* come across the line "For saints have hands, blah, blah, blah." We have been rehearsing this production of Romeo and Juliet for eight weeks. *Eight weeks*, Miss Priestly, out of which you missed *three*.

MEREDITH. I was in Aruba. Working on my tan.

MS. CHENAULT. *(at the same time)* …working on your tan… Yes, I know.

MEREDITH. Duh.

MS. CHENAULT. Subtract three from eight and what do you have remaining, Miss Priestly?

MEREDITH. *(thinking)* Duh…five.

MS. CHENAULT. Yes, "duh" five. Brava, Miss Priestly. Very good. Five. Five weeks in which you were to learn your lines.

MEREDITH. I haven't had time. I have a life…

MS. CHENAULT. *(saying the word "life" at the same time)* …life. Yes, I know, Miss Priestly. I, too, have a life, Miss Priestly – the theatre. The theatre is my life. We open this classic love story; a story of unrequited passion; a story of two star crossed lovers; *Romeo and Juliet* in just…

MEREDITH. *(interrupting)* Why are we even doing Romeo and Juliet anyway? What does that have to do with Christmas? We should be doing something with a Christmas theme like *A Christmas Carol.* Why aren't we doing *A Christmas Carol?*

MS. CHENAULT. Because, Miss Priestly, *everyone* does *A Christmas Carol* this time of year; which is why *we* are doing *Romeo and Juliet,* which we open in just two days – in two days, Miss Priestly; forty-eight hours – and our Juliet. Does. Not. Know. Her. Lines.

MEREDITH. I'll just use cue cards.

(Holding in her rage, **MS. CHENAULT** *turns to the other cast members.)*

MS. CHENAULT. That's all for this afternoon, ladies and gentlemen. Please remember to hang up your costumes *neatly* and replace all props to their *proper* place on the prop table. Melissa, will you please check in everyone's costume?

MELISSA. Yes, ma'am.

(Everyone, sensing the tension, exits. **MEREDITH** *starts to cross with them.)*

MS. CHENAULT. Miss Priestly, I would like a word with you, please…

EVERYONE ELSE. *(as they are exiting)* "Oooohhhhh…."

MEREDITH. *(imitating)* "Ooooohhhh…"

(After everyone has exited, **MEREDITH** *and* **MS. CHENAULT** *are alone onstage. There is silence.)*

MEREDITH. *(to* **MS. CHENAULT** *)* What?

MS. CHENAULT. Miss Priestly…

MEREDITH. It's no big deal. You can make the cue cards at home. You've got two days.

MS. CHENAULT. I'm not going to be making any cue cards, Miss Priestly.

MEREDITH. You're not?

MS. CHENAULT. No.

MEREDITH. Fine. It's your funeral.

(**MEREDITH** *starts to exit.*)

MS. CHENAULT. I'm not through with you.

(**MELISSA** *stops and turns to* **MS. CHENAULT.**)

MEREDITH. What?

(**MS. CHENAULT** *slowly begins to cross toward* **MERE-DITH.**)

MS. CHENAULT. Throughout this entire rehearsal process – throughout this entire year, you have been nothing but disrespectful and irresponsible. Do you realize how difficult it is to be a teacher, Miss Priestly?

MEREDITH. You buy chalk. How difficult can that be?

MS. CHENAULT. Apparently you don't. Athough teaching brings great rewards, it also brings great challenges.

MEREDITH. I plan on having a real job.

(*pause…*)

MS. CHENAULT. And as a teacher it is my responsibility to impart upon my students a sense of pride and respon-sibility. And in the theatre – especially in the theatre, I cannot allow one person's nonexistent work ethic to affect the progress of others.

(*beat*)

Do you know what I am saying, Miss Priestly?

MEREDITH. Oh, I'm having my mother replace my costume with something from Versace.

MS. CHENAULT. Replace? Interesting word choice, Miss Priestly. For I, too, am replacing something.

MEREDITH. Please say it's your hair color.

MS. CHENAULT. No, Miss Priestly. You.

MEREDITH. What?

MS. CHENAULT. You. I am replacing you.

MEREDITH. You mean in the play?

MS. CHENAULT. Yes, Miss Priestly. In the play.

MEREDITH. As Juliet?

MS. CHENAULT. Yes. As Juliet.

MEREDITH. You can't do that!

MS. CHENAULT. I believe I can.

MEREDITH. We open in two days. Who are you going to find to play Juliet in two days?

MS. CHENAULT. Melissa Barclay. She knows the lines.

(pause)

MEREDITH. I wouldn't do this if I were you.

MS. CHENAULT. You wouldn't?

MEREDITH. Nope.

(beat)

Let me ask you something, Ms. Chenault. When you walk into the theatre, on the front of the building in large, looming stone letters, what do you see?

(beat)

You see the name "Josiah Priestly Theatre." And who is Josiah Priestly? Oh, that's right! *My grandfather.* Who is also the *mayor,* and the father of my father who is *President of the school board!* And we're rich. Filthy, stinking rich. So I can do pretty much anything I want. Capeche? So I don't think you'll be making any "changes," Ms. Chenault; unless, of course, you want to find yourself teaching Shop next semester.

(She starts to exit then stops.)

Oh, and you better get cracking on those cue cards. You've only got forty eight hours.

(beat)

Merry Christmas.

*(**MEREDITH** exits on a disbelieving **MS. CHENAULT,** who is speechless. Lights fade to black as the music rises.)*

Scene Two
Cheerleading Practice, West End High School

(During the blackout the set pieces from the rehearsal scene are struck and two benches which are placed end to end downstage are brought on. As the scene change music fades we hear…)

CHEERLEADERS.

HEDGEHOG FANS SHOW YOUR SPIRIT!
YELL OUT LOUD SO WE CAN HEAR IT!
HEDGEHOG SPIRIT!
HEDGEHOG SPIRIT!
HEDGEHOT SPIRIT!
THAT'S IT FANS YOU'VE GOT IT RIGHT!
SHOW YOUR SPIRIT FOR THE GREEN AND WHITE!
GREEN AND WHITE!
GREEN AND WHITE!
GREEN AND WHITE!
THAT'S IT FANS HELP US OUT!
LOUDER NOW LET'S HEAR YOU SHOUT!

YAY!

(The **CHEERLEADERS – LYDIA IVEY, TIFFANY BAINBRIDGE, MELISSA BARCLAY,** *and* **SERENA FAIN** *– complete their cheer with the requisite jumping up and down, etc. Then in the calm which follows some rest on the benches, others on the floor. Some stretch – others take a sip from their water bottles, etc…)*

TIFFANY BAINBRIDGE. Hey, Lydia – where's Meredith?

MELISSA. I dunno. I saw her in French.

TIFFANY. That's weird. She never misses cheerleading.

LYDIA. Maybe Ms. Chenault gave her detention.

MELISSA. Nah. I saw her after rehearsal, and she didn't say anything about getting detention. Although she should have.

SERENA FAIN. *(to* **MELISSA***)* Why don't you call her?

MELISSA. Lost my cell.

SERENA. I heard Ms. Chenault let her have it.

MELISSA. More like Meredith let Ms. Chenault have it. I heard some of it from backstage. I can't believe the way she spoke to her. A teacher. An adult. It was unbelievable. I wonder what her parents would do if they knew she treated adults like that?

SERENA. Meredith's parents aren't around enough to know what goes on. They just give her a credit card, a thousand dollars in cash, catch a plane for Europe, and leave her by herself.

TIFFANY. What did Meredith say to Ms. Chenault?

MELISSA. Meredith told her she'd do whatever she wanted because of her grandfather and her father, and because she's rich.

LYDIA. No kidding?

MELISSA. *And* told Ms. Chenault that if she wasn't careful, she'd find herself teaching Shop next semester!

SERENA. Ms. Chenault should just kick Meredith out and replace her in the play.

TIFFANY. Replace her in the play? It opens tomorrow! There's no way Ms. Chenault could find someone that quickly. No way!

SERENA. If I knew the part *I* could play it. I'm a great actress.

LYDIA. Melissa knows it. She could do it. Couldn't you, Melissa?

MELISSA. I'm just the stage manager.

LYDIA. But you've been there every rehearsal! You probably know *everyone's* lines! Ms. Chenault would be stupid *not* to let you do it, if she had to.

(There is a pause. **MELISSA** *looks around to see if anyone is eavesdropping.)*

MELISSA. I'm going to tell you guys something, but you have got to promise *not* to tell anyone else.

(beat)

Promise?

EVERYONE. *(ad libs)* "Yeah, we promise," "Sure," "I don't tell secrets," etc…

MELISSA. Green and White promise?

> (**EVERYONE** *"nods yes." The Green and White Promise is something they reserve for very serious situations so there is an elaborate hand ritual which accompanies the agreement to seal the pact.)*

SERENA. Ok. Tell.

MELISSA. When I got home last night…

TIFFANY. *(interrupting)* How's your sister?

MELISSA. Better, thanks…

SERENA. Go on.

MELISSA. When I got home last night Ms. Chenault called me and talked to me about…being Juliet.

SERENA. NO!

LYDIA. Melissa, you'd be *perfect* for it! You're a *much* better actress than Meredith.

TIFFANY. You kidding? My short haired chihuahua is a better actress than Meredith.

SERENA. What did you say to her?

MELISSA. I couldn't do that to Meredith! She's my best friend! I couldn't take Juliet away from her!

TIFFANY. Melissa, I've seen her act. She stinks.

LYDIA. P.U.

SERENA. And you wouldn't be *taking* the part away from her. Ms. Chenault *asked* you to, didn't she?

MELISSA. Yeah. Pretty much. She did. But I could tell she was afraid, too. After Meredith threatened her, y'know. She's scared of her.

TIFFANY. She scares me, that's for sure.

LYDIA. Nevermind that. I am *so* excited about the elementary school Christmas party tomorrow!

SERENA. It's my favorite part of Christmas! Melissa, that was a great idea of yours for the cheerleading team to host it. Absolutely perfect.

MELISSA. *(shyly)* Thanks.

TIFFANY. I've been helping them with their Christmas play!

MELISSA. It's going to be great! I've got all kinds of games planned, caroling – the works!

(From the back of the theatre we hear…)

MEREDITH. AND SPEAKING OF WORK, IT'S SO REFRESHING TO SEE MY SQUAD *NOT* WORKING! NO WONDER OUR CHEERLEADING TEAM IS THE WORST IN THE DISTRICT!

LYDIA. Meredith! We were just taking a break. We've been practicing!

MEREDITH. *(as she comes down the aisle and comes onstage)* Taking a break? Taking a break? There is no time for breaks! The championship is just four months away. PRACTICE! PRACTICE! GET ON YOUR FEET! FORMATION!

(**EVERYONE** *jumps up and gets into their previous cheer line again.)*

MEREDITH. AND GO!

EVERYONE. *(Except* **MEREDITH** *who paces up and down the formation reviewing her "troops." As the* **GIRLS** *are cheering,* **MEREDITH** *is offering ad libbed critiques, i.e., "Kick higher!," "Louder," "Stand up straight," etc.)*
HEDGEHOG FANS SHOW YOUR SPIRIT!
YELL OUT LOUD SO WE CAN HEAR IT!
HEDGEHOG SPIRIT!
HEDGEHOG SPIRIT!
HEDGEHOG SPIRIT!
THAT'S IT FANS YOU'VE GOT IT RIGHT!
SHOW YOUR CHEER FOR THE GREEN AND WHITE!
GREEN AND WHITE!
GREEN AND WHITE!
GREEN AND WHITE!
THAT'S IT FANS HELP US OUT!
LOUDER NOW LET'S HEAR YOU SHOUT!
YAY!

(The **GIRLS** *complete their cheer then anxiously turn toward* **MEREDITH** *for her verdict. There is a pause.)*

MEREDITH. Apparently we're going to have to double up practices.

(The **GIRLS** *moan…)*

I mean *triple* the number of times we practice. That was sloppy, lazy, and just plain gross.

(to **MELISSA***)*

It seems I am unable to trust our Co-Captain to keep you in shape while I'm not here.

LYDIA. Meredith, we don't have time to practice. We've got school, homework, the play, and the kids Christmas party we're sponsoring.

MEREDITH. Getting this team in shape is more important than handing out candy canes to a room full of snot nosed brats!

(The school bell rings. Grateful for the opportunity to escape, the **GIRLS** *quickly gather their things and start to exit as* **MEREDITH** *continues…)*

It's my responsibility as Captain for you not to make a fool out of me. So I expect to see some improvement immediately, or else you're off the team. ALL OF YOU!

(The **GIRLS** *continue to exit.)*

(becoming suddenly coldly sweet) Oh, Melissa – I have something for you.

MELISSA. What?

*(***MEREDITH** *reaches into her backpack and withdraws a cell phone.)*

MEREDITH. This.

MELISSA. My cell! Thanks. Where did you find it?

MEREDITH. You left it in French class.

MELISSA. Did my sister call?

MEREDITH. No. But someone else did. They left a voice mail.

(beat)

Which, of course, I listened to. Being the kind and caring person I am.

MELISSA. Oh. Uh. Thanks.

MEREDITH. Don't you want to know who it was?

MELISSA. No. I'll listen to it later.

MEREDITH. It was Ms. Chenualt. Now why would Ms. Chenault call you?

MELISSA. It was probably something about the play. A costume or a prop. Something.

MEREDITH. Oh, it *was* something, alright. About the play. A little something about…

(imitating Ms. Chenault)

"Melissa, it's Ms. Chenault, again. I was wondering if you had made a decision about what we talked about earlier – about your taking over Juliet? Call me back, please."

(There is a pause. The cat is out of the bag…)

MELISSA. Meredith, it wasn't my idea.

MEREDITH. Oh, I know it wasn't *your* idea. Because any idea you have, *I* give you.

MELISSA. I wouldn't take Juliet away from you. You're my best friend.

MEREDITH. Oh, I know you wouldn't. Otherwise, you'd no longer be my "best friend," and you know what happens to people who are no longer my "best friends"?

MELISSA. No.

MEREDITH. And you wouldn't want to.

(beat)

Now you call Ms. Chenault and tell her you have no intention of being Juliet.

(The school bell rings again.)

MELISSA. *(nervously)* I gotta go. I'll. Be. Late. Y'know?

(**MELISSA** *starts out then stops.*)

Oh. By the way – what are you doing for Christmas?

MEREDITH. What?

MELISSA. What are you doing for Christmas? Your parents are going to be in Nairobi, aren't they?

MEREDITH. Yeah.

MELISSA. You're welcome to spend it with us. Liz and I. If you want.

(There is a pause.)

I gotta go.

(beat)

See ya tomorrow.

(**MEREDITH** *doesn't respond as* **MELISSA** *exits and the lights fade to black.*)

Scene Three
Meredith's Bedroom

(During the blackout the benches in the previous scene are struck and a bed is rolled on. Beside the bed is a nightstand on which rests a phone. **MEREDITH** *enters with her designer bag and her Juliet cone hat. She throws them on her bed and checks the answering machine.)*

ANSWERING MACHINE. *(the voice of* **MEREDITH'S FATHER***)* Meredith, it's mumsie and popsie. We leave on safari tomorrow morning, so if you need anything, call Mr. Foster at the bank and he will take care of it. We will see you in two weeks.

(the voice of **MEREDITH'S MOTHER***)*

Oh, and darling, sweetie – be a lamb and call Dr. Harris and have him Federal Express me a vial of Botox, sweetie, darling. This African heat is making my face fall like the walls of Jericho, sweetie, darling.

(both voices)

Oh, and darling, sweetie, sweetie, darling – Merry Christmas!

*(***MEREDITH** *switches off the answering machine. She exits then quickly reenters with a bag of Cheetos. She takes out her laptop from her designer bag and crawls into bed. She then "fires up" her computer, and unconsciously begins munching on her Cheetos. After a moment when the computer has "loaded," she begins typing. She is completely concentrating on her computer when she hears a banging noise offstage. She looks up, startled. She looks offstage right – seeing nothing she returns to her work. After a moment a LOUD banging noise is heard followed by a clap of thunder, and the lights suddenly to go black.)*

MEREDITH. *(in the black)* Great…

(We hear the strains of ominous music as the lights dimly rise to a "spooky" blue as fog rolls in…)

MEREDITH. *(cont.)* *(to herself)* What is going on?

(The music grows louder – the smoke grows thicker – **MEREDITH** *grows more apprehensive…)*

Who's there? WHO'S THERE!?!

(With a flash and a musical flourish **GWENDOLYN CHESWICK** *appears through the smoke, choking and coughing.* **MEREDITH** *grabs her designer bag and clutches it to her.* **GWENDOLYN** *is dressed recognizably from the Victorian period and sporting fairy wings. Her bodice and skirt are weighed down with all manner of things – chains, boxes, etc…She blindly stumbles into the room. Upon seeing her* **MEREDITH** *screams…)*

MEREDITH. *(screaming)* Aaaaaaahhhhhhhhhhhhhhhh….!

*(***GWENDOLYN***, equally startled, screams also…)*

GWENDOLYN. Aaaaaaahhhhhhhhhhhhhhhh…!

MEREDITH. WHO ARE YOU?!? GET OUT OF HERE?!?

*(***GWENDOLYN***, disoriented due to the excessive smoke, stumbles about the room, coughing, choking and fanning the smoke away from her…)*

GWENDOLYN. *(to* **MEREDITH** *and through her coughing)* You know, that smoke gets more difficult to regulate each time.

MEREDITH. What?

GWENDOLYN. The smoke. I hate it. I'm required to use it, y'know. Regulation 2 dash B 4 7: "All entities making an appearance on the earthly plane are required to utilize the special effect of smoke upon their entrance." I hate it. Stinks, too.

(She remembers something.)

Oh – just a sec.

*(***GWENDOLYN** *reaches into her coat pocket and withdraws a small notebook. She rapidly flips through the pages, obviously looking for something…)*

MEREDITH. I'm calling the police.

GWENDOLYN. *(She stops on a page – reads for a moment then looks up at* **MEREDITH**.*)* You're not Gladys Twiddlebaum, are you…?

MEREDITH. Uh. No.

GWENDOLYN. I didn't think so. You don't look like a Gladys.

(**GWENDOLYN** *returns to her notebook, flipping furiously through its pages.)*

MEREDITH. Who are you?

GWENDOLYN. *(holding up her finger as if to indicate "just one moment, please)* What's your name?

MEREDITH. Meredith.

GWENDOLYN. *(continuing her page flipping)* Last name?

MEREDITH. Priestly.

GWENDOLYN. *(as she attempts to find her name on her "list")* Priestly…Priestly…Priestly…

(She stops as she has found her information.)

Ah, yes – there you are.

(She looks more closely at the page.)

Oh, no. This isn't good.

(She looks up at **MEREDITH**.*)*

Boy howdy. You're mean.

MEREDITH. Look…

GWENDOLYN. *(She returns to her reading.)* I mean, you're really, really, really mean. Not nice at all.

(beat)

Yuck!

MEREDITH. *Who are you?*

(**GWENDOLYN** *tucks her notebook into her skirt and twirls about the room, her arms in fifth position.)*

GWENDOLYN. Gwendolyn Cheswick, at your service, madam! Ghost extraordinaire from "the world beyond." My card.

(**GWENDOLYN** *presents* **MEREDITH** *with her business card.*)

MEREDITH. *(with disbelief as she takes the card)* Yeah. Right.

GWENDOLYN. No, really.

MEREDITH. *(reading the card)* A "ghost"?

GWENDOLYN. I prefer the term "friendly spirit," but that cost extra, and there wasn't room on the card.

(beat)

I'm cheap.

MEREDITH. *(eyeing how **GWENDOLYN** is dressed)* Evidently in the "world beyond" all ghosts shop at Uncle Bob's Bargain Barn.

(beat)

So what's with the wings?

GWENDOLYN. It's how I fly. Duh.

MEREDITH. Like the Tooth Fairy?

GWENDOLYN. The Tooth Fairy?!? Don't mention that name to me. I *hate* her. I called her last week for lunch – I never heard back from her. She's dead to me.

(**GWENDOLYN** *spits on the ground.*)

MEREDITH. Gross. You are *so* cleaning that up.

(There is a pause.)

GWENDOLYN. You don't believe me, do you?

MEREDITH. Nope.

GWENDOLYN. Uh. Why not? You have my card! You can see me…

MEREDITH. And smell you…

GWENDOLYN. *(insulted)* HEY!

(beat and as though reciting a rehearsed line complete with indicative arms) "The evidence is before you, yet you do not believeth." Why?

MEREDITH. Because you could be anything.

GWENDOLYN. Anything?

MEREDITH. A dream, perhaps. Or with those clothes you're wearing, more like a nightmare. I'm probably in my bed, dead to the world simply dreaming. Or I could've swallowed a Cheeto the wrong way, and I'm hallucinating. Or you might be…

(*GWENDOLYN* *raises a frightful cry and races around the room making all manner of "ghostly noises." Taken aback,* **MEREDITH** *joins in the screaming…*)

Okay! Okay! Okay! I get it! You're a ghost. Boo! Scary! I GOT IT!

(**GWENDOLYN** *calms down and sits at the foot of the bed.*)

Now. What are you doing here?

GWENDOLYN. I have come to warn you.

MEREDITH. About what?

GWENDOLYN. Just a sec.

(*She reaches into the waist of her skirt and withdraws her small notebook again. She opens it and reads*)

"It is required of every man that the spirit within him should walk abroad among his fellow-men, and travel far and wide; and if that spirit does not go forth in life, it is condemned to do so after death."

(*beat*)

MEREDITH. (*having absolutely no idea what she just heard means*) Huh?

GWENDOLYN. Sorry. I was supposed to memorize that, but I have trouble memorizing things.

MEREDITH. Yeah. I hear ya, sister.

(*a quick "high five"*)

What are all of these things on your clothes? Chains and stuff? You need better accessories.

GWENDOLYN. Oh. Well…y'see, when I was alive I was…

MEREDITH. (*interrupting*) Wait – "when you were alive?"

GWENDOLYN. Yeah. I'm *dead.* That's why I'm a *ghost.* And when I was *alive,* I am embarrassed to say, I was just as mean as you. *Meaner,* in fact – if that's even possible. And these chains and boxes and empty tomato juice cans...

(perhaps directly to the audience)

...all of which are recyclable...

(back to **MEREDITH***)*

...weigh me down, and are the result of my being so nasty for so long to everyone and everything.

(rising to stand on top of the bed as she adopts a "scary and ominous" voice)

And unless you...

(She glances back down at her notes, then in her regular voice:)

...Meredith Preistly...

(She looks back up at **MEREDITH** *and resumes her "scary and ominous" voice. VERY, VERY melodramatically building as this moment was previously rehearsed to death.)*

"...change your ways, you, too, shall be doomed to wander the earth for all of eternity weighed down by the chains your nasty, awful, mean spirited, vindictive, ways!"

MEREDITH. *(doubtfully)* Seriously?

GWENDOLYN. Oh yeah.

(beat and returning to the melodrama)

BUT, "you have yet a chance and hope of escaping my fate, Meredith Priestly!"

(There is a pause.)

MEREDITH. Okay. I'll bite. How?

GWENDOLYN. *(once again...the melodrama)* "You will be haunted...by Three Spirits! Without their visits, you cannot hope to shun the path I tread. Expect the first tomorrow, when the bell tolls One."

MEREDITH. Couldn't they all just come at once? I do have a life, you know.

GWENDOLYN. *(and the melodrama continues)* "And expect the second on the next night at the same hour. The third upon the next night when the last stroke of Twelve has ceased to vibrate. Look to see me no more; and look that, for your own sake, you remember what has passed between us."

(We hear a cell phone ring. **MEREDITH** *immediately starts to look for hers.* **GWENDOLYN***, likewise, searches for hers. Each take out their respective phones…)*

GWENDOLYN. *(to* **MEREDITH***)* It's me.

(answering her phone)

Hello?

(There is a pause.)

Yes…yes…okay…no, I'm just about to wrap up here…. Sure…I can pick up some milk on my way in…a gallon…2%…got it…and Poptarts…Cherry…

(She hangs up her phone.)

Gotta run. That was Casper. We're kinda dating.

(beat then for the last time – with melodrama)

"REMEMBER WHAT I'VE SAID!"

(returning to her normal voice)

See ya.

(out to the back of the theatre)

CUE SMOKE! CUE MUSIC!

(The smoke billows onstage as the music rises and **GWENDOLYN** *disappears. Once she is gone the music fades, the lights return to normal and the smoke dissipates.* **MEREDITH** *stands looking where* **GWENDOLYN** *was just a moment before. Then, out to the audience…)*

MEREDITH. Okay. *That* was odd.

*(***MEREDITH** *crosses to her bed and crawls in.)*

Stupid Cheetos.

*(***MEREDITH** *turns and goes to sleep as the lights fade.)*

Scene Four
Meredith's Bedroom

(All is quiet and restful. **MEREDITH** *sleeps soundly. Suddenly* **GWENDOLYN** *appears holding a handheld gong. She strikes it once – the stroke of one!* **GWENDOLYN** *disappears.* **MEREDITH** *awakes with a start. We then hear the sounds of a football band.* **GWENDOLYN** *pokes her head around the stage right proscenium arch and to the back of the house.)*

GWENDOLYN. CUE SMOKE!

(The smoke pours on stage as the music continues. We then hear from off stage right…)

PATTY & PATRICK PRINCE. *(cheering)*
HEY! HEY! HEY! HEY! HEY! HEY!
GET UP LAZY BONES AND GET OUTTA BED!
ONE WOULD THINK THAT YOU WERE DEAD!
WE'RE HERE TO TAKE YOU BACK TO YOUR PAST!
SO GET UP, GET DRESSED AND LET'S HAVE A BLAST!

*(***PATTY*** *and* ***PATRICK*** *ad lib as they jump up and down, strike Cheerleading poses. However, from their dress, it is obvious they were cheerleaders in another time. Startled,* **MEREDITH** *has jumped up from her sleeping position and is now standing on the bed at the head of it.)*

MEREDITH. Okay, okay, okay…what's the deal here? Who are *YOU*!

PATTY. Oh…dears. Did Gwenie not tell you of our visit?

PATRICK. Oh, that Gwenie! She's *such* a butter brain!

PATTY. *(to* **PATRICK***)* "Butter brain!" You said "butter brain!"

(She starts to giggle uncontrollably.)

You are *so* funny!

PATRICK. I know, I *am* funny.

PATTY. *(to* **MEREDITH***)* Isn't he funny?

(beat)

He kills me.

MEREDITH. "Gwenie" *did* mention something about a visit, but she mentioned only ONE ghost.

PATRICK. We come as a pair.

PATTY. "Two for one!"

(**GWENDOLYN** *appears onstage and blows a whistle, which* **PATTY** *and* **PATRICK** *take notice of as an indication to move on.)*

PATTY & PATRICK. *(striking a cheerleader pose)* LET'S GO!

PATRICK. SO! You ready to make like a banana and split?

(**PATTY** *giggles uncontrollably again.)*

PATTY. *(to* **PATRICK***)* You are SO funny!

PATRICK. I know. I *am* funny.

PATTY. If we were still alive, I'd vote for you for class clown.

PATRICK & PATTY. *(to* **MEREDITH** *as they come forward to get her)* So…LET'S GO!

PATTY. We're on a schedule, you know!

MEREDITH. *(backing away)* Whoa, whoa, whoa, whoa – wait just a second. I'm not going anywhere with you! I don't even *know* you!

PATRICK. *(to* **PATTY***)* She's right!

PATTY. *(to* **PATRICK***)* What a coupla duddle brains we are!

(as **PATTY** *and* **PATRICK** *cross to* **MEREDITH** *with their hands outstretched for a handshake)*

I'm Patricia Penelope Prince. But you can call me Patty.

PATRICK. And I'm Patrick Paul Prince. But you can call me Patrick.

PATTY. We were once cheerleaders at West End High.

PATRICK. Many, many years ago!

PATTY & PATRICK. CLASS OF 1956! WHEN ELVIS AND POODLE SKIRTS WERE ALL THE RAGE!

(They both perform a hurkey cheerleading jump.)

YAY! US!

(They stick their hands out to **MEREDITH** *for a handshake once more.)*

MEREDITH. *(reluctantly taking shaking their hands)* Hello.

(beat)

Gross.

(She wipes her hands on her pants.)

PATRICK. Well, now that we're all introduced...

PATTY. ...and the swellest of friends...

PATTY & PATRICK. ALL ABOARD AND LET'S GO!

*(***PATTY*** and **PATRICK** *sweep forward and on either side hook their arms through* **MEREDITH**'s, *who is obviously offended by the smell.)*

MEREDITH. *(reacting to the stench)* Does everyone in the afterlife stink?

PATRICK. Pretty much. We're dead.

PATTY. Here we go!

MEREDITH. Wait! Wait! WAIT! Where are we going?

PATRICK. Why to the past, of course!

MEREDITH. Whose past?

PATTY. *Your* past, silly goose!

MEREDITH. I can't go to the past! I've got cheerleading and shopping and...stuff.

PATRICK. But we must go to the past so you can see why you've become such a brat!

PATTY & PATRICK. GO, BRATS!

(They strike a cheerleading pose.)

PATTY. Come and let us fly!

(**PATTY** *and* **PATRICK** *lead* **MEREDITH** *up to her bed on which they all three stand.*)

MEREDITH. We better be traveling first class!

(**PATTY, PATRICK** *and* **MEREDITH** *jump off the bed onto the stage. The lights change instantly and cheerful music begins to play.*)

Where are we?

(*From offstage we hear giggling and laughter. A* **LITTLE MEREDITH** *runs on stage from stage right crossing down to the opposite side. After a moment, a group of young* **BOYS** *run in behind her. They stop midway. The little girl and the group of young boys freeze as the lights change to isolate* **PATTY**, **PATRICK**, *and* **MEREDITH**.*)

PATTY. Do you recognize this place?

MEREDITH. *(mystified)* Yeah. It's the playground of my elementary school.

(*The lights change to full wash as the* **BOYS** *come forward and begin to taunt* **LITTLE MEREDITH**.*)

BRUNO. Hey guys! The principal must've changed the rules and allowed *DOGS* to come to school!

(*The boys cruelly laugh.*)

ACE. Yeah – don't get too close or we'll get rabies!

(*The boys cruelly laugh again.*)

LITTLE MEREDITH. Shut up!

MEREDITH. *(to* **PATTY** *and* **PATRICK***)* Is that little girl *me*?

PATTY & PATRICK. *(striking a Cheerleader pose)*
Yyyyeeeesssssssssss, ma'am!

ROGER. Hey, Meredith! I hear you're…

(in baby talk)

…"gwanna hav to spwend your wittle birfday all wonesome, cause you pawents are in Engwand."

LITTLE MEREDITH. That's not true! I'm NOT all alone. Mr. Foster from the bank is bringing me stuff.

ACE, BRUNO & ROGER. *(ad libbing)* "Yeah," "Right," "I just bet"…

LITTLE MEREDITH. Well, he is! He's bringing me cake and ice cream and *lots* of presents. HUNDREDS!

ACE. Yeah, right.

BRUNO. We believe you.

ROGER. Sure he is.

LITTLE MEREDITH. It's true!

> *(The **BOYS** laugh.)*

You're just jealous because my Daddy's super rich and your Daddies are super poor.

(reversing the taunting)

"Oh, look at me! I wear hand-me-down clothes!," "Look at me, I live in a trailer!" Blah, blah, wah, wah, wah! "I'm poor! I'm dirty! I'm gross!"

BRUNO. YOU TAKE THAT BACK!

LITTLE MEREDITH. I WON'T.

ROGER. TAKE IT BACK!

LITTLE MEREDITH. NO!

> *(A fight breaks out with ad libs. One would think **LITTLE MEREDITH** would be overpowered by three boys, but she easily holds her own. There is much yelling, much scuffling…)*

MEREDITH. *(to **PATTY** and **PATRICK**)* Do something!

PATTY & PATRICK. *(chanting as though this is a cheer)* INTERFERENCE, BETWEEN THEM AND YOU! INTERFERENCE, WE CAN NEVER DO!

> *(**PATTY** and **PATRICK** strike a cheerleader pose.)*

GO TEAM!

> *(Suddenly **LITTLE MELISSA** runs in.)*

LITTLE MELISSA. STOP IT! LEAVE HER ALONE!

> *(**LITTLE MELISSA** inserts herself into the scuffle, pulling the **BOYS** and **LITTLE MEREDITH** apart.)*

LITTLE MELISSA. *(cont.)* Get on outta here before I tell the principal!

(The **BOYS** *begin to taunt* **LITTLE MELISSA.***)*

THE BOYS. *(ad libbing)* "Tattle tale! Tattle tale!," "Narc!," "Why don't you go blab it to your mommy?"

LITTLE MELISSA. I just might! And I'll blab it to *your* mommies, too! How would you like that? Huh?

(She makes a threatening move…)

Now get outta here!

(The **BOYS** *don't move.)*

(making another threatening move) GO ON!

(The **BOYS***, sufficiently afraid now, run offstage.* **LITTLE MELISSA** *watches them leave, then turns to* **LITTLE MEREDITH***.)*

Are you okay?

LITTLE MEREDITH. Yeah. I'm fine. I didn't need your help.

LITTLE MELISSA. Yeah, you did.

PATTY & PATRICK. AAAAAAAANNNNNNNNNNNDD DDDDDDDD, FREEZE!

*(***PATTY** *and* **PATRICK** *strike another cheerleader pose as* **LITLE MEREDITH** *and* **LITTLE MELISSA** *freeze.* **MEREDITH** *looks upon them, deep in thought, then…)*

MEREDITH. *(to* **PATTY** *and* **PATRICK***; softening a bit)* Melissa took up for me…?

PATTY. You forgot? Of course she took up for you. She *is* your best friend, isn't she?

(There is a pause.)

MEREDITH. Yeah. Sure.

(Beat. Hardening again:)

She's a pansy.

*(***GWENDOLYN** *appears onstage and blows her whistle, which is a signal for* **PATTY** *and* **PATRICK** *to move on.)*

PATTY & PATRICK. *(once again in a "cheer chant)*
YOU CAN'T STAY HERE AND BE A SPECTATOR!
WE MUST MOVE ON TO A FEW YEARS LATER!
LET'S GO!

> *(**LITTLE MEREDITH** and **LITTLE MELISSA** run offstage as the lights change. As they are running offstage, we hear laughter and festive ad libs as **LYDIA**, **MELISSA**, **TIFFANY**, and **SERENA** excitedly enter, dressed rather nicely, as the "dance" music swells. **MEREDITH**, **PATTY**, and **PATRICK** cross to the opposite side of the stage. Music which will underscore the following…)*

SERENA. I am *so* nervous!

LYDIA. Me, too – we are going to have such a B-L-A-S-T tonight!

ALL. A BLAST!

> *(The **GIRLS** break out into a gale of giggles; jumping up and down, etc.)*

TIFFANY. Our first boy-girl dance! It's going to be the bomb! THE BOMB!

> *(The **GIRLS** break out into another gale of giggles; jumping up and down, etc.)*

MEREDITH. *(to **PATTY** and **PATRICK**)* It's the Winter Dance last year!

PATTY & PATRICK. *(as a cheer)* GOOOOOOO, WINTER!

> *(The strike a cheerleader pose as **MELISSA** enters and strikes a fashion model pose.)*

MELISSA. Hello, girls!

> *(The girls turn and see **MELISSA**, who is stunning!)*

TIFFANY. Oh, Melissa! You look FABULOUS!

LYDIA. That dress is beautiful! I love it!

SERENA. Where did you get it?

MELISSA. My sister made it!

ALL. *(ad libbing)* "You are kidding me!," "It looks fantastic!," "That's amazing!," etc.

MELISSA. Do you think Bolt will like it?

(**BILLY, MONTY** *and* **MELVIN** *enter.*)

BILLY. *(to* **MELISSA***) I* sure do! You look HOT!

MELISSA. *(giggling)* Thank you, Billy. You look very handsome, too.

(to the rest of the boys)

ALL of you do!

(Embarrassed, but pleased, the **BOYS** *look down at their feet with "aw shucks" ad libs.)*

I can't believe Bolt Lancaster, *the* hottest guy on campus *and* a *Senior* asked *me* to this dance! *This is going to be the greatest night ever!*

(The **GIRLS** *squeal with excitement as the music grows louder.)*

TIFFANY. *(squealing with excitement)* IT'S THE FIRST DANCE!

(The **GIRLS** *scream with delight, jumping up and down, as the* **BOYS** *check their appearance. With the* **BOYS** *on one side of the stage and the* **GIRLS** *on the other, the* **GIRLS** *look at the* **BOYS** *with expectant anticipation to be asked to dance. The* **BOYS** *are uncertain what to do as the* **GIRLS** *look eagerly on. The* **BOYS** *push* **MELVIN** *out ahead.* **MELVIN** *nervously crosses to the* **GIRLS** *and approaches* **LYDIA***.)*

MELVIN. *(His voice cracks.)* Lydia...

(He stops, coughs and tries again in a markedly put upon deeper voice.)

Lydia. Would you care to dance?

*(***LYDIA** *turns back to the* **GIRLS** *who are looking on. They all scream with delight.)*

LYDIA. *(turning back to* **MELVIN***)* Yes. Thank you.

*(***LYDIA** *offers her hand, which* **MELVIN** *takes and leads her across stage where they find a spot and begin to dance. Once they begin to dance, the other* **BOYS** *bravely approach the other girls.)*

BILLY. Tiffany, would you care to…

TIFFANY. *(interrupting)* YES!

> *(**TIFFANY** forcibly grabs **BILLY**, drags him across stage, and they begin to dance. **MONTY** approaches **SERENA**.)*

MONTY. Serena? Wanna boogie?

SERENA. YOU BET I DO!

> *(**SERENA** starts after **MONTY**, then stops.)*

> *(to **MELISSA**)*

Melissa? You gonna be okay?

MELISSA. Of course! Bolt, *my* dreamboat, should be here any minute. Go on!

> *(**SERENA** and **MONTY** cross the stage and begin dancing.)*

PATTY & PATRICK. ANNNNNDDDD FREEZE!

> *(Everyone on stage freezes, the music stops and there is a light change.)*

PATTY. *(to **MEREDITH**)* Do you remember what happened next?

MEREDITH. *(reluctantly)* Not really. It was last year.

PATRICK. I think you do.

> *(There is a pause.)*

PATTY. *(indicating **MEREDITH** should enter the scene)* Go on.

MEREDITH. I don't want to.

> *(There is a pause.)*

PATRICK. We're waiting.

MEREDITH. *(protesting)* I don't have to do anything I don't want to! I'm rich!

PATTY. If you don't, we'll be stuck here forever.

PATRICK. So you kinda *have* to.

> *(**PATRICK** hands **MEREDITH** a wrist corsage and realizing she has no choice, steps into the scene. Instantly the music returns, the lights brighten and **MEREDITH** is transformed into herself a year prior. **MELISSA** notices her.)*

MELISSA. Meredith! There you are! You look beautiful!

MEREDITH. Yes. I know. It's Dolce & Gabanna.

(**MEREDITH** *notices* **MELISSA***'s dress.*)

Where did you get that?

MELISSA. *(proudly turning and modeling for her)* My sister made it.

MEREDITH. Really? I didn't realize this was a costume party.

(**MEREDITH** *breezes past* **MELISSA***, who is hurt for a moment, then decides to "suck it up.")*

MELISSA. I hope Bolt likes it. He said it was his favorite color.

MEREDITH. He's not coming.

MELISSA. Not coming? What do you mean?

MEREDITH. Simple. He's not coming.

(The others onstage hear this, stop dancing and watch and listen as the music fades in volume a bit.)

MELISSA. Of *course* he's coming. He's *my* date!

MEREDITH. *Was* your date. I saw him this afternoon and he realized he'd have a much better time with me at our lake house while my parents are in Prague, than with you here at this little "kiddie" dance. I have the chauffeur waiting – we're leaving now.

MELISSA. You're kidding…

MEREDITH. No. I'm not.

(Pause as **MELISSA** *realizes* **MEREDITH** *is not kidding.)*

MELISSA. Meredith! How can you do this? I'm your best friend!

MEREDITH. Yeah. Right.

(calling offstage)

I'll be right there, Bolt!

MELISSA. *(realizing)* You're serious.

MEREDITH. I am.

(pause)

MELISSA. If you're going away with Bolt, why did you come by here?

MEREDITH. To rub it in, of course.

(beat)

Ciao!

(as she is leaving)

I'll call you on Monday and tell you all about our weekend.

*(**MEREDITH**, with a flourish, "exits," but before she truly exits the stage, she turns and assumes the attitude of the present **MEREDITH** and crosses back to **PATTY** and **PATRICK** while watching the continuing action.)*

*(**MELISSA** watches where **MEREDITH** made her "exit" and fights not to cry. A fight she fails to win. The others, who have been watching the entire time, feel awkward. **TIFFANY** comes forward.)*

TIFFANY. Melissa? You okay?

MELISSA. *(through her tears as the music rises)* How could she do that? How could…*I'm* her best friend! I don't understand how…

*(The others, uncertain what to do, look at each other uncomfortably. **LYDIA** nudges **MELVIN** forward. He cautiously approaches **MELISSA**. He glances back over his shoulder to **LYDIA**, who encourages him.)*

MELVIN. *(to **MELISSA**)* Melissa? Would you care to dance?

MELISSA. *(still looking after where **MEREDITH** made her "exit")* No.

(beat)

Thank you.

*(**MELVIN** crosses back to **LYDIA**, shrugging his shoulders. The **COUPLES** slowly return to dancing as the lights dim as they rise on **MEREDITH**, **PATTY** and **PATRICK**. As the music contines to play the **COUPLES** dance off and **MELISSA** exits as the scene continues…)*

(**MEREDITH**, *in the present, is visibly affected by what she has just seen and participated in.*)

PATTY. *(commenting on what they have just witnessed)* Golly.

PATRICK. Golly, indeed.

MEREDITH. I can't believe I did that. I can't believe I stole her date.

(**GWENDOLYN** *appears again and blows her whistle.* **PATTY** *and* **PATRICK** *look at each other and begin to cheer as they, with* **MEREDITH** *in tow, begin to move across stage.*)

PATTY & PATRICK. *(as a cheer)*
WE'VE HEARD THE WHISTLE, IT'S TIME TO FLY!
YOU'LL MISS US, TRUE; BUT PLEASE DON'T CRY!
THE NEXT GHOST COMES; BUT NO NEED TO FEAR IT!
BECAUSE YOU'VE GOT 1950's SPIRIT!

(By this time **PATTY** *and* **PATRICK** *have transported* **MEREDITH** *back to her bed.* **MEREDITH,** *hidden by* **PATTY** *and* **PATRICK,** *crawls into the bed and pulls the covers up around her as though she's been sleeping. Once there* **PATTY** *and* **PATRICK** *turn back to the audience.)*

GO TEAM!

(They strike a cheerleading pose followed by a quick blackout. After they exit in the dark, the lights dimly rise and we find **MEREDITH** *in her bed, asleep. There is a pause, then she wakes with a start.)*

Scene Five
Meredith's Bedroom

MEREDITH. *(waking – startled)* Ohhh!

(pause as she looks around the room to orient herself)

Okay. *That* was a weird dream.

(beat)

Stupid Cheetos.

(The answering machine kicks on automatically.)

ANSWERING MACHINE. *(voice of* **MEREDITH'S MOTHER***)*

Darling poopsie poo – it's mother! Listen, darling! *HUGE* disaster! You must call Dr. Harris *immediately* and have him over night some collagen to me, darling! This African heat has dried up my lips! They are literally *collapsing* on top of each other! I look a *fright*! *Thanks* everso, darling. Merry Christmas!

*(***MEREDITH*** glances at the answering machine, pauses for a moment. She then refluffs her pillow and returns to sleep.)*

MEREDITH. *(to herself)* I *hate* Christmas.

*(The lights dim slightly as the music rises. **MEREDITH** turns over in her bed – a quick indication of a passage of time.)*

*(***GWENDOLYN*** suddenly appears with a handheld gong, which she strikes once and disappears. **MEREDITH** stirs for a moment, then falls back to sleep. Suddenly there is a bright light from behind and steping out of the light, wearing sunglasses, is **LILLIPUT**, a sprite and the Ghost of Christmas Present. **LILLIPUT** enters the room and finds the sleeping **MEREDITH**. Disgusted she crosses to the bed and slaps **MEREDITH**'s feet under the covers.)*

LILLIPUT. Wake up!

*(***MEREDITH*** mumbles, but doesn't stir.)*

(slapping her feet with a bit more force) WAKE UP, I SAID!

(**MEREDITH** *bolts upright from the pain.*)

MEREDITH. OUCH! Watch it. I just had a pedi!

(*beat*)

Who are you?

LILLIPUT. You *know* who I am.

MEREDITH. (*realizing it's the next ghost*) Oh. Right. You.

LILLIPUT. (*slyly waving*) Hello!

MEREDITH. (*sleepily*) Now which one are you?

LILLIPUT. *I* am Lilliput, the sprite of Christmas Present! NOT to be confused with the Ghost of Christmas *Presents*, which is an entirely different thing altogether.

MEREDITH. So you're not a ghost?

LILLIPUT. I'm a sprite.

MEREDITH. A sprite?

LILLIPUT. No thank you, I prefer Dr. Pepper.

(**LILLIPUT** *cracks up in laughter at her own joke.*)

You walked into that one, didn't you? Admit it – you walked into that one!

MEREDITH. Okay. Yes. I walked into that one.

LILLIPUT. Oh, that joke never gets old.

(**LILLIPUT** *starts to laugh again as* **GWENDOLYN** *appears with the gong, which she strikes once, then disappears.*)

Oh! We gotta get outta here! Got things to do, places to go and people to see! (*grabbing* **MEREDITH** *out of bed*) Come on!

MEREDITH. Wait! Wait!

(**LILLIPUT** *stops.*)

LILLIPUT. What?

MEREDITH. Look – do we *really* have to do this tonight? I *really* learned a lot last night – learned my lesson, so if we could just skip this tonight I could get some sleep, and…

(**LILLIPUT** *twirls* **MEREDITH** *in a series of circles as they cross the stage, which makes* **MEREDITH** *very, very dizzy.*

MEREDITH. *(as she is being spun)* Whoa!

(They twirl then suddenly stop.)

LILLIPUT. *(grandly)* Well – here we are!

MEREDITH. Where?

*(***LILLIPUT***, confused, looks around.)*

LILLIPUT. Hmmm. Strange. They are supposed to here.

MEREDITH. Who?

LILLIPUT. Excuse me.

*(***LILLIPUT*** crosses the stage.)*

Gwenie?

*(***GWENDOLYN*** appears.)*

GWENDOLYN. Yes?

LILLIPUT. Uh. Sorry to bother…

GWENDOLYN. It's alright.

LILLIPUT. But we have an itsy-bitsy problem, here.

GWENDOLYN. An "itsy-bitsy problem"? Oh, dear, that's not good, now is it?

LILLIPUT. No it isn't. You see, the problem is…

*(***LILLIPUT*** suddenly changes from sweet sprite to spiteful sprite.)*

THE SCENE ISN'T HERE!

*(***GWENDOLYN*** is taken aback by this sudden outburst.)*

GWENDOLYN. Oh. Yes. Dear me. Well, let me see what I can do about that.

LILLIPUT. PLEASE DO!

GWENDOLYN. Excuse me…

*(***GWENDOLYN*** skitters offstage. Once gone, **LILLIPUT** turns back to **MEREDITH**, who is a bit afraid of this side of* **LILLIPUT**.*)*

LILLIPUT. *(explaining)* We sprites, as a species, have an anger management problem. I'm in therapy.

(beat)

They should be along in a moment.

(There is an awkard pause.)

So…

(beat)

Yeah.

MEREDITH. So…uh…what exactly is a sprite?

LILLIPUT. A caffeine free soft drink!

*(**LILLIPUT** cracks up, once again, at her own joke.)*

I tell you! I tell you! That *never* gets old!

MEREDITH. It does. Believe me. And quickly.

*(From offstage we hear the ad libs of a party. **GWENDOLYN** appears.)*

GWENDOLYN. They're coming!

*(**GWENDOLYN** disappears as **LYDIA**, **TIFFANY**, **SERENA**, **MELVIN**, **BILLY** and **MONTY** enter. They are carrying boxes of decorations, snacks, etc. **LILLIPUT** and **MEREDITH** back out of the way to observe.)*

LYDIA. Party time, guys!

TIFFANY. *(to **MELVIN**, **BILLY** & **MONTY**)* Thanks guys, for helping us out on such short notice!

BILLY. No sweat!

SERENA. Yeah – the little kids are going to love it!

MELVIN. Need some help decorating?

LYDIA. Yeah.

MELVIN. Cool.

(beat)

C'mon Monty.

*(**MONTY** and **MELVIN** start to help decorate, and everyone else joins in.)*

MEREDITH. *(to* **LILLIPUT***)* What is this?

LILLIPUT. The elementary school Christmas party *you* are supposed to be volunteering for.

MEREDITH. Oh. That.

SERENA. It's too bad Melissa couldn't make it. She was so excited about it.

LYDIA. How's her sister?

MEREDITH. *(to* **LILLIPUT***)* What's wrong with her sister?

LILLIPUT. What do you care? She's a "pansy," remember?

MEREDITH. How did *you* know I called her that?

LILLIPUT. We see all. We hear all. We know all.

(back to the scene…)

TIFFANY. It doesn't look good.

SERENA. Geez. That's too bad.

LYDIA. What about Meredith?

BILLY. *(laughing)* Meredith? Yeah, right! Like *she'd* be here.

MELVIN. Yeah! She's probably off to…

(imitating **MEREDITH***'s voice and walk)*

…Paris…

MONTY. *(also imitating* **MEREDITH***)* …or Rome…

BILLY. *(joining in with his own imitation)* …or London…

MONTY. *(still imitating)* "Oh, look at me! Aren't I gorgeous! Look at how rich I am!

(The **GIRLS** *start to laugh. The laughter from everyone builds throughout.)*

BILLY. *(still imitating)* "Look at me! Look at how fabulous I am. Don't you wish you were me!"

LYDIA. *(doing her imitation)* "Look at me! Aren't I *stupendous?* I'm dating Prince William!"

MELVIN. *(still imitating)* "I'm having my Daddy clone me so I can date myself!"

TIFFANY. *(doing her imitation)* "Look at me! Jealous? You should be!"

SERENA. *(doing her imitation)* "Hey! Hey! Look at me! I'm the most beautiful, the most talented, the most *hated* girl in school!"

BILLY. Hey…guys, listen to what Melvin made up about Meredith! It's hilarious!

MONTY. Yeah – do it, Melvin.

MELVIN. *(still imitating)* "My daddy has a plane! My mother has a yacht! My parents are wherever I am not!" *

*(Everyone breaks up in laughter. **LILLIPUT** interrupts.)*

LILLIPUT. Aaaaaaaaaaaaaaaaannnnnnnnnnnnnnddddddddd dddd, FREEZE!

*(Everyone onstage freezes as the lights change. There is a pause as **MEREDITH** looks on in complete shock. She walks among her frozen "friends"; **LILLIPUT** stays put.)*

MEREDITH. Wow.

(beat)

That's what they *really* think of me?

LILLIPUT. Surprised?

MEREDITH. Yeah. I am.

(beat)

I mean, I was.

LILLIPUT. Until you *heard* yourself…

MEREDITH. Yeah. And *saw* myself.

LILLIPUT. Sometimes you have to take a step back. See yourself as others see you.

MEREDITH. Yeah.

(beat)

You do.

LILLIPUT. Aaaaannnnnnnnnnnnnnnnddddddd GO!

*(Instantly the lights brighten, Christmas music begins to play and the stage springs to life with **MEREDITH** caught in the middle of it. The others ignore her presence as she really isn't there. The others, who were frozen earlier in*

---

*For an optional replacement scene that does not contain younger, child actors, please refer to the APPENDIX at the end of the play.

mid laugh, pick up their laughter. From offstage we hear an excited cheer.)

LYDIA. HERE THEY COME!

(A group of small children run onstage screaming, thoroughly and completely excited.)

THE GANG. *(except the young kids) (ad libs)* "Hey, there!," "Merry Christmas!," "It's a party!," "Aren't you excited?," etc.

LYDIA. *(trying to be heard over the din of the children)* Okay. Okay! OKAY!

(The children quieten.)

We are SO excited you guys are here tonight!

THE CHILDREN. *(cheering)* YAY!

SERENA. We're going to play games!

BILLY. Have snacks!

TIFFANY. Sing carols!

MONTY. And have TONS OF FUN!

LYDIA. But first some little sprite told me…

    *(**MEREDITH** looks at **LILLIPUT**.)*

LILLIPUT. Wadn't me.

LYDIA. …that you guys have a Christmas play to perform for us!

TIFFANY. That's right, they've been working very, very hard!

THE CHILDREN. *(cheering)* YAY!

LYDIA. So let's get this party started with…YOUR PLAY!

THE CHILDREN. *(cheering)* YAY!

TIFFANY. *(helping arrange the children in their position for their play)* Okay. You guys get set.

*(As the children are getting arrange in their places, a child (**ISAAC**) comes up to **TIFFANY**.)*

ISAAC. Miss Tiffany?

TIFFANY. Yes, Isaac?

ISAAC. Where's Miss Melissa?

THE OTHER CHILDREN. *(ad libbing)* "Yeah, where's Miss Melissa?," "Why isn't she here?," "Is she sick?," etc.

TIFFANY. *(addressing the children)* Miss Melissa's sister is very, very sick. She had to stay home and take care of her. So you need to keep Miss Melissa and her sister in your thoughts, ok?

THE CHILDREN. *(ad libbing)* "Yes," etc…

TIFFANY. And Miss Meredith won't be able to be here, either.

SARAH. That's okay. We don't like her. She's mean.

JOHN DAVID. Yeah. Who cares about *her*!

(Everyone but the children stifle their laughter.)

MELVIN. *(energetically interrupting)* I don't know about you guys, but I am ready to see a play!

THE CHILDREN. *(cheering)* Yay!

*(The **CHILDREN** take their places to begin their play as the others sit down on the stage floor to be their audience. **TIFFANY** remains with the **CHILDREN** as their Director.)*

TIFFANY. *(addressing the "audience")* Ladies and Gentlemen, the West End Elementary After School Drama Club proudly presents for your viewing pleasure, a Christmas classic for all ages.

*(The "audience" wildly applauds and yells for the **CHILDREN**.)*

Go on, Violet.

*(A little girl, **VIOLET**, stands up.)*

VIOLET. Thank you for attending our production this evening. We'd like to remind you that the use of flash photography during this evening's presentation is strictly prohibited. Please turn off all cell phones, pagers and handheld devices. Thank you.

*(**VIOLET** takes her place so the play may begin.)*

TIFFANY. And now, Ladies and Gentlmen, Boys and Girls, I give you "The Night Before Christmas."

(more applause)

ISAAC. T'was the night before Christmas, when all through the house,

Not a creature was stirring, not even a mouse.

STEPHANIE. The stockings were hung by the chimney with care,

In hopes that Saint Nicholas would soon be there.

JOHN DAVID. The children were nestled all snug in their beds,

While visions of sugar plums danced in their heads.

SARAH. And mama in her 'kerchief, and I in my cap,

Had just settled down for a long winter's nap.

MICHAEL. When out on the lawn there arose…

ALL OF THE CHILDREN. SUCH A CLATTER!

MICHAEL. I sprang from my bed to see what was the matter.

(**MEREDITH** *crosses and sits with the others in the "audience" to watch the performance.*)

JULIE. Away to the window I flew like a flash,

Tore open the shutters and threw up the sash.

JEREMY. The moon on the breast of the new-fallen snow,

Gave the luster of mid-day to objects below.

ISAAC. When what to my wondering eye should appear,

But a miniature sleigh and eight tiny reindeer.

VIOLET. With a little old driver so lively and quick,

That I knew in a moment it must be St. Nick.

JOHN DAVID. More rapid than eagles his coursers they came,

And he whistled, and shouted and called them by name.

SARAH. Now, Dasher!

MICHAEL. Now, Dancer!

JULIE. Now, Prancer and Vixen!

JEREMY. On, Comet! On Cupid!

ALL OF THE CHILDREN. On, Donder and Blitzen!

ISAAC. And then, in a twinkling, I heard on the roof,
The prancing and pawing of each little hoof.

VIOLET. As I drew in my hand, and was turning around.
Down the chimney St. Nicholas came with a bound.

JOHN DAVID. A bundle of toys he had flung on his back,
And he looked like a peddler just opening his pack.

SARAH. He spoke not a word, but went straight to his work,
And filled all the stockings, then turned with a jerk.

MICHAEL. And laying his finger aside of his nose,
And giving a nod, up the chimney he rose.

JULIE. He sprang to his sleigh, to his team gave a whistle,
And away all they flew like the down of a thistle.

JEREMY. But I heard him exclaim, ere he drove out of sight,

ALL OF THE CHILDREN. MERRY CHRISTMAS TO ALL, AND TO ALL A GOOD NIGHT!

(Tumultuous applause and shouts of approval from the "audience," as the **CHILDREN** *take their bows.)*

TIFFANY. That was outstanding. BRAVO!

SERENA. *So* outstanding that I think that performance deserves LOTS of ICE CREAM and other stuff that isn't good for you!

EVERYONE. *(including* **MEREDITH***) (cheering)* YAY!

SERENA. COME ON GUYS! LET'S PIG OUT!

*(***SERENA*** leads the way offstage as everyone else, including* **MEREDITH** *follow, cheering.)*

EVERYONE. YAY!

(As **MEREDITH** *starts to run off to join the party,* **LILLIPUT** *stops her…)*

LILLIPUT. Where do you think *you're* going?

MEREDITH. To join the party.

LILLIPUT. No.

MEREDITH. But they're so cute!

LILLIPUT. I recall you describing them "snot nosed brats"…

MEREDITH. How did you…?

LILLIPUT. *(interrupting)* We hear all and…

LILLIPUT & MEREDITH. See all.

LILLIPUT. Besides, you aren't really here, remember?

> *(beat)*

> Come. We have one other stop to make. Come.

> *(The lights dim as **LILLIPUT** places her arm around **MEREDITH***'s shoulders to guide her as music underscores. As the lights rise on the opposite side of the stage, we find **ELIZABETH BARCLARY**, **MEREDITH***'s ill sister, in a wheelchair with a lap blanket and the receiver of a cordless phone in her lap. She is asleep. **MEREDITH** turns and notices her.)*

MEREDITH. *(to **LILLIPUT**)* Who's that?

LILLIPUT. Don't you recognize her? That's Melissa's sister.

MEREDITH. *(shocked at her appearance)* She looks really bad.

LILLIPUT. She's been ill for a very long time.

> *(From offstage we hear…)*

MEREDITH. I didn't know.

LILLIPUT. Yes you did. You just didn't care.

MELISSA. *(from offstage)* Liz?

> *(**MELISSA** enters carrying a glass of water, a couple of pills and a candle. She crosses to **ELIZABETH**.)*

> Liz?

> *(Seeing **ELIZABETH** is asleep, **MELISSA** gently wakes her.)*

> Liz. Wake up.

> *(**ELIZABETH** groggily stirs.)*

> Here. It's time for these.

> *(**MELISSA** gives **ELIZABETH** the capsules and the glass of water. **ELIZABETH** takes the pills and gives the water back to **MELISSA**, which she sets down.)*

MELISSA. *(cont.) (as she is tucking in* **ELIZABETH** *'s blanket around her legs)* How are you feeling?

ELIZABETH. Better. I think. Better.

MELISSA. Why do you have the phone with you?

ELIZABETH. In case I need to make a call.

(noticing the candle)

What's with the candle?

MELISSA. What?

ELIZABETH. Candle. The candle. What's with the candle?

MELISSA. Oh. I just thought it was Christmas-y. That's all.

(beat)

Can I get you anything?

ELIZABETH. No. Thank you.

*(***MELISSA** *starts to exit.)*

These trailers are so cold! Melissa, turn up the heat.

*(***MELISSA** *stops – hesitates.)*

What's wrong?

(laughing)

You forget to pay the electric bill?

*(***MELISSA** *hesitates.)*

MELISSA. No. I paid it. I sent your check last week.

(beat)

It bounced.

*(***ELIZABETH** *says nothing; embarrassed.)*

I tried to talk them into extending it – give us more time, but they said no. After the second shut off notice, they have to.

ELIZABETH. "They have to." They have to watch us freeze to death. I'll call them tomorrow and get it straightened out.

MELISSA. The phone's been turned off, too.

(beat)

I'm sorry.

(pause)

ELIZABETH. No. No. *I'm* sorry.

*(**ELIZABETH** reaches out for **MELISSA**.)*

C'mere.

*(**MELISSA** takes **ELIZABETH**'s hand and sits at her feet in front of the wheelchair.)*

I am so sorry for so many things.

(beat)

Sorry about Dad leaving. Mom dying. Sorry I'm sick. Sorry you have to take care of me. Sorry we're poor.

(beat)

Sorry about a lot of things.

MELISSA. I don't mind.

ELIZABETH. *I* do. You should be out with your friends. Not here, with me – in this icebox of a trailer. Stuck out here in the middle of nowhere. No neighbors. No one to talk to but me.

(beat)

The children's party's tonight.

MELISSA. Yes.

ELIZABETH. You were looking forward to it.

MELISSA. I'd rather be here with you.

ELIZABETH. No. You wouldn't. You shouldn't. You *should* be with your friends.

MELISSA. I couldn't leave you here by yourself. You need me.

ELIZABETH. Yep. I do.

(beat)

Here.

(She takes out a small wrapped package from underneath her lap blanket.)

It's just a little something.

MELISSA. But it's not Christmas yet.

ELIZABETH. I wanted to give it to you early.

(beat)

Just in case. Y'know.

(**MELISSA** *studies* **ELIZABETH**, *knowing what she means.)*

Go ahead and open it.

(**MELISSA** *unwraps her present and upon opening the box, discovers it's a bracelet.)*

MELISSA. It's beautiful…

ELIZABETH. It was Mom's. I don't know if it's worth any money, but it's priceless to me.

MELISSA. *(She puts the bracelet on.)* Thank you, Liz. I love it.

(She then looks out front.)

Oh, look! It's snowing.

(pause)

I love the snow. So fragile. So peaceful.

(beat)

Do remember the Christmas when we lived on Crestview drive…? I was eight – maybe nine; before Daddy left. Before Mom…And Meredith and I built that enormous snowman. You took pictures.

(**ELIZABETH** *has fallen asleep.)*

We were so proud. And then the sun came out, and he melted – and I cried and cried and cried. Meredith called me a pansy. And you held me close, kissed my forehead and said, "Sometimes things fade away in this world, but that doesn't mean you'll never see them again."

(beat)

You remember that, Liz?

(There is no response.)

Liz…you remember that Christmas?

(Still, no response. **MELISSA** *turns to her)*

MELISSA. *(cont.)* Liz? You asleep?

(Beat. **MELISSA** *gently tries to rouse* **ELIZABETH.***)*

Liz – wake up.

(Beat. **MELISSA** *realizes something is wrong and more forcibly attempts to wake her up.)*

Liz? LIZ?!?

(to herself as she grabs the phone and starts to dial, panicked)

No, no, no, no, no…

(She then realizes the phone is dead and hurls it to the floor.)

LIZ! LIZ! LLLLLLLLIIIIIIIIIIIIZZZZZZZZZZZ!

(The lights fade out on **MELISSA** *and* **ELIZABETH***; they freeze.)*

MEREDITH. *(to* **LILLIPUT***)* DO SOMETHING!

LILLIPUT. There's nothing I *can* do.

MEREDITH. You're a sprite! A magical creature, right? You can do anything! DO SOMETHING! *Stop time – cast a spell;* SOMETHING!

LILLIPUT. I told you, there's nothing I *can* do.

MEREDITH. SHE'S DYING! SHE'S ALL MELISSA HAS!!!

*(***MEREDITH** *is completely stunned; speechless. She crosses over to the frozen* **MELISSA** *and* **ELIZABETH** *and studies them.)*

No. It's not fair. Not to Melissa. She's so…kind. Loving. Thoughtful. Strong.

LILLIPUT. Not a pansy…?

MEREDITH. *Not* a pansy.

(There is a clap of thunder then the errie sound of wind. The lights dim, **MELISSA** *and* **ELIZABETH** *exit. From the opposite side of the stage, a hooded figure dressed completely in black from head to toe, enters in a haze of fog. This is the* **GHOST OF CHRISTMAS FUTURE.** **LILLIPUT** *notices them.)*

LILLIPUT. Ah. There you are. Right on time, as usual. She's all yours.

*(Beat. Then to **MEREDITH**)*

See ya.

*(**LILLIPUT** starts to exit. **MEREDITH** stops her.)*

MEREDITH. Wait! Where are you going?!?

LILLIPUT. My time's up, m'dear.

MEREDITH. *(indicating where **MELISSA** and **ELIZABETH** were before)* But what about…

LILLIPUT. Think about this, Meredith. Just think. Of all the people in Melissa's life, who is the one who could make the most difference…? Think.

MEREDITH. I don't…

LILLIPUT. You.

MEREDITH. What difference could *I* make?

LILLIPUT. A very, very valuable one.

(beat, then cheerfully)

Well, I'm off. Goodbye and good luck!

(She turns to leave then remembers)

Oh, by the way this is the Ghost of Christmas Future. Future, Meredith – Meredith, Future.

*(**DEATH** waves.)*

Adios.

*(And with a curtsey, **LILLIPUT** exits.)*

MEREDITH. *(calling after her)* Thank you.

*(**LILLIPUT** reenters.)*

LILLIPUT. *(disbelieving)* Did you just say "thank you?"

MEREDITH. Yes.

(beat)

Thank you.

LILLIPUT. Wow. Guess my night wasn't a waste afterall!

*(**LILLIPUT** starts to exit again. **MEREDITH** stops her.)*

MEREDITH. Oh…this hanging out with this Future thing. I *guess* I have to do this, huh?

LILLIPUT. 'Fraid so. But don't worry, he won't bite.

(beat)

Too hard.

*(**MEREDITH** reacts.)*

I'm kidding!

(beat)

Bye!

*(**LILLIPUT** exits.)*

MEREDITH. *(calling after her, weakly…)* …bye..

*(Left alone with death, **MEREDITH** is understandably nervous.)*

Boy, do I dread you.

(attempting a compliment)

You look good in black.

*(There is no reaction from **FUTURE**.)*

Wow. Tough room.

(beat)

Okay. Let's do this.

*(**FUTURE** begins to cross, with **MEREDITH** following…)*

Where are we going…?

*(The "answering machine" kicks on and we hear the voices of **MEREDITH'S FATHER** and **MOTHER**, once again.)*

MEREDITH'S FATHER. *(voiceover)* Darling, it's father. Mother and I are calling from the airplane enroute to Kenya. Listen, poopsie, do Mother a favor and call Mr. Don and have him overnight her hair extensions.

MEREDITH'S MOTHER. *(voiceover)* Yes, sweetie, darling – I simply MUST have them. They will look stunning on me when I wear them on the Savannah tomorrow, darling.

MEREDITH'S FATHER. *(voiceover)* And, darling, please call Mr. Foster at the bank tomorrow and have him open a line of credit for us at...

(On the voiceover we hear a BANG! **FUTURE** *continues to cross the stage with* **MEREDITH** *following.* **TWO PEOPLE** *enter, also dressed in black carrying something behind their backs. They cross upstage and stop.)*

MEREDITH'S MOTHER. *(voiceover)* What was that?

(We hear the sounds of an airplane out of control and screams.)

AIRPLANE CAPTAIN. *(voiceover)* Ladies and gentlemen, we please ask that you return to your seats and fasten your seat belts. Flight Attendants, please prepare for an emergency landing...

MEREDITH'S MOTHER. *(voiceover)* Harold, what's happening...?

MEREDITH'S FATHER. *(voiceover)* I don't know...

(There is the sound of an enormous explosion. Then all is quiet. The **TWO PEOPLE** *turn and we see they are each holding a tombstone.* **MEREDITH** *looks back at* **FUTURE** *fearfully.* **FUTURE** *points for* **MEREDITH** *to read the tombstones. With dread and somewhat knowing what to expect, she approaches the tombstones and reads them.)*

MEREDITH. *(reading the tombstones)* "Harold and Cynthia Priestly."

(back to **FUTURE***)*

They're dead. Plane crash?

*(***FUTURE** *nods "yes.")*

But...what happens...to me? I'd be an orphan. Like Melissa! I have no other family. I know they're gone a lot. All the time, but they're my parents, and...what happens to me?

*(***FUTURE** *points to the opposite side of the stage, a* **BEGGAR WOMAN** *darkly dressed with a shawl over her head, enters. As* **MEREDITH** *watches, she crosses to her;*

holding out her hand for money. **MEREDITH** *recoils from her…backing up as the* **BEGGAR WOMAN** *follows.)*

MEREDITH. *(cont.)* Who are you? Go away! You stink. Leave me alone.

(The **BEGGAR WOMAN** *continues to approach* **MEREDITH** *who continues to back away until* **MEREDITH** *is pushed back on her bed. At this point the* **BEGGAR WOMAN** *rips off her shawl and we see it's* **MEREDITH**. **MEREDITH** *screams…*

MEREDITH. *(screaming)* Aaaaaaahhhhhhhhhhhh…!

(There is a blackout. The **BEGGAR WOMAN** *and* **FUTURE** *exit in a clap of thunder. There is a pause. During the blackout,* **MEREDITH** *returns to a sleeping position under the covers. The lights slowly rise.* **MEREDITH** *awakes with a start. She looks around her thinking, "Am I alive?," "Am I still here?." When she realizes she is indeed, she starts to laugh. The answering machine kicks on…)*

MEREDITH'S FATHER'S VOICE. *(voiceover)* Darling, sweetie, it's Daddy, could you please…

*(***MEREDITH** *grabs the phone punching "talk," which turns off the answering machine…)*

MEREDITH. *(into the phone)* Daddy?…Are you and Mom okay?…No…I just…I just had a bad dream and…I miss you…What?…How was the play?…

(She laughs.)

I don't know. I slept right through it…What? What do you mean it opens today? The play was yesterday…. No, they didn't move the date…I just…wait…what's the date?…You're kidding!?!…I didn't miss it!…It IS TODAY!…You're what?…You are seriously flying in to see it?…That's terrific!…I gotta go. I gotta get to the theatre. I LOVE YOU!

*(***MEREDITH** *hangs up the phone, grabs the phone book, furiously flips through and finds what she's looking for. She dials the number…)*

MEREDITH. *(cont.)* Is this Meader's Antique Books…?

   (blackout)

Scene Six
The Stage at West End High School

(In the dark we hear a commotion, a frenzy – and as the lights rise we see **MELVIN, MONTY, BILLY, LYDIA, MELISSA, TIFFANY** *and* **SERENA** *dressed as they were in the first scene. It is opening day of* Romeo and Juliet. **MS. CHENAULT,** *who is "fit to be tied," enters.)*

MS. CHENAULT. Any luck?

MELISSA. I've called her cell phone six times. No answer.

MS. CHENAULT. Keep trying. And when she does show up, send her immediately to me. Oh, and Melissa, you better get in costume.

MELISSA. Yes, ma'am.

*(***MELISSA*** exits as* **MS. CHENAULT** *exits opposite.)*

BILLY. I can't believe Meredith would screw up the entire production!

TIFFANY. Don't worry – the show will go on. Melissa can do Juliet.

SERENA. And she'll do a *much* better job!

LYDIA. I don't think I want to be around when Meredith finds out Ms. Chenault took Juliet away from her.

MONTY. She's gonna FLIP OUT!

(From the back of the theatre we hear…)

MEREDITH. *(cheerfully)* Hey, guys!

*(***MEREDITH*** bounds down the aisle with a large package in her hand and wearing her Juliet cone hat.)*

MELVIN. IT'S MEREDITH!

BILLY. RED ALERT! RED ALERT!

SERENA. *(running offstage)* MS. CHENAULT! MEREDITH'S HERE! MS. CHENAULT!

MEREDITH. You guys look great!

TIFFANY. What…? Where have you been?!? You're an hour LATE! The curtain is about to go up!

MONTY. Ms. Chenault is going to kill you!

TIFFANY. That's it, Meredith Priestly – I have had it! You are the most selfish, self-absorbed, self-centered, thoughtless, cold-hearted, back-stabber I have ever known. And I don't care if you DO kick me off the squad, I don't want anything more to do with you! What do you think of that?

(There is a pause. The others are stunned by **TIFFANY***'s rant.* **MEREDITH** *stands before her, staring her down, then throws her arms around her and gives her a big hug.)*

MEREDITH. I think you're absolutely wonderful!

*(***TIFFANY** *is stunned.)*

TIFFANY. *(backing away)* Are you trying to stab me?

MEREDITH. *(laughing)* Of course not! I just wanted to give you a hug – that's all.

TIFFANY. Why…? *Who* are you?

MONTY. Here comes Ms. Chenault.

*(***MS. CHENAULT** *enters followed by* **MELISSA.** **MEREDITH** *has her back to her. Everyone else backs away from the line of fire.)*

MS. CHENAULT. MISS PREISTLY! SO YOU FINALLY DECIDED TO SHOW UP! THAT'S VERY GRACIOUS OF YOU CONSIDERING THE CURTAIN GOES UP IN LESS THAN AN HOUR TO A SOLD OUT HOUSE! WHERE HAVE YOU BEEN? OH, THAT'S RIGHT, YOU HAVE A LIFE?!? I HAVE A CHRISTMAS PRESENT FOR *YOU*, MISS PRIESTLY.

MEREDITH. *(turning to face* **MS. CHENAULT** *with package in hand)* AND I HAVE ONE FOR YOU!

*(***MS. CHENAULT** *eyes* **MEREDITH** *and the package suspiciously.)*

MS. CHENAULT. Is that a bomb?

MEREDITH. Open it.

*(***MS. CHENAULT** *is frozen, uncertain if she should.)*

Go on.

(**MS. CHENAULT** *looks around at the others, stil uncertain. Then slowly and cautiously she begins to unwrap the package. When the wrapping is off we can see it is a book.* **MS. CHENAULT** *stares at the cover, speechless.*)

MS. CHENAULT. I don't believe it...

(beat)

Is this really...?

MEREDITH. Yes. One of Shakespeare's folios.

(beat)

Original.

MS. CHENAULT. Uh...thank you. But...

MEREDITH. Why? Well, because...you like Shakespeare and...

(**MEREDITH** *notices everyone staring at her.*)

Listen. Guys. I've been a terrible friend. Who am I kidding – I haven't been a friend at all! I've said terrible things about you – to your face and behind your backs. You're right, Tiffany – I am selfish, self-centered, all of those things you said. And I am so sorry. To all of you. And I hope you can forgive me.

SERENA. Is this a trick?

MEREDITH. I don't blame you for being suspicious. I would be, too. But something wonderful happened. Something wonderful, and frightening and overwhelming and beautiful.

(**MEREDITH** *notices* **MELISSA.** *She crosses to her.*)

Melissa Barclay...

(beat)

...first off, how's your sister?

MELISSA. *(stunned* **MEREDITH** *is asking)* Uh...she's fine. Better. Thank you. Thank you for asking.

MEREDITH. That's a relief.

(Beat. She takes **MELISSA***'s hands into her own.)*

Melissa Barclay. You have been a true friend to me. And I have treated you like a dog. You have been kind, loyal, caring and thoughtful. And I have treated you like a dog. You have been compassionate, self-sacrificing, patient and selfless. And I have treated you like a dog. Please, please, please, Melissa – please, please forgive me. I am *so* sorry for the way I have treated you over the years. I am so fortunate and grateful to have a friend like you; *if* you will *be* my friend.

*(***MELISSA*** is thoughtful for the moment.)*

MELISSA. I won't be your friend. I'll be your *best* friend.

(They hug.)

MEREDITH. And I'm going to have my dad call Dr. Harris first thing tomorrow, and get your sister the best care my father's tons of money can buy. And I'll have him call Mr. Foster at the bank and get you out of that trailer!

MELISSA. Aren't they in Nairobi?

MEREDITH. Not anymore. They're flying in to see the play!

LYDIA. I am really freaked out confused here.

BILLY. Meredith, are you serious about all of this?

MEREDITH. I am. Very serious. And I am very serious about asking for your forgiveness.

(beat)

Can you…all of you, please forgive me? And let me be a true friend?

(Everyone looks at **MEREDITH**, *then at each other. They are cautious – debating her sincerity. Finally* **MS. CHENAULT** *steps forward.)*

MS. CHENAULT. Miss Priestly.

> *(beat)*

> Meredith…I can see something significant has happened to you. A miracle, perhaps? We all deserve the chance to make things right. We all deserve another try – another opportunity. You've given everyone here, including me, just cause to doubt everything you're saying. You'll have to prove yourself. It will take time. But I believe it will be time well spent. And *if* you are sincere, then yes, I forgive you.

BILLY. Me, too.

MONTY. Me, too.

MELVIN. Ditto.

LYDIA & TIFFANY. Why not?

SERENA. Sure.

MEREDITH. Thank you. All I can ask for is a chance…right?

MS. CHENAULT. Right.

> *(beat)*

> Now, ladies and gentlemen, we have a show to do.

> *(ad libs of excitement)*

> Five minutes to places.

> *(additional ad libs of excitement as the actors prepare)*

> Meredith, may I speak with you, please…

MEREDITH. Ms. Chenault, before you say anything, I have a terrific idea.

MS. CHENAULT. Meredith, I am the director, so *all* ideas should come from…

MEREDITH. I think Melissa should play Juliet!

MS. CHENAULT. *(taken aback)* What?

MEREDITH. She's a much better actress than I am *and* she *knows* the lines.

MS. CHENAULT. Well…uh…ALRIGHT!

MEREDITH. Great!

> *(crossing to stage right shouting into the wings)*

> MELISSA!

> **(MELISSA** *enters dressed in black and wearing her head-set.)*

MELISSA. You need something?

MEREDITH. No. But *you* do.

MELISSA. No. I'm fine.

MEREDITH. No, you're not. You can't go on as Juliet without *this.*

> **(MEREDITH** *takes off her Juliet cone hat and places it on* **MELISSA***'s head.)*

MELISSA. What are you doing?

> *(beat)*

> Ms. Chenault?

MEREDITH. *(as she takes* **MELISSA***'s headset)* And *I* can't tell you when to make your entrance, without this!

MELISSA. But…I couldn't…I can't…

> *(beat)*

> Can I, Ms. Chenault?

MS. CHENAULT. Not only can you. You *will!*

MELISSA. But, I…

MEREDITH. Melissa, I stink as an actress. I do. P.U. And you're *great.* And you know the lines and you fit the costume…so go. GO!

> **(MELISSA** *gives* **MEREDITH** *a great big hug then runs offstage, excitedly.)*

MS. CHENAULT. *(smiling and pleased…)* One point for Meredith Priestly.

> *(beat – as she is crossing to exit)*

> OK PEOPLE! WE'VE GOT A SHOW TO DO. *PLACES!*

(**MEREDITH** *starts out.* **GWENDOLYN** *enters, followed by* **LILLIPUT, PATTY, PATRICK** *and* **FUTURE.**)

GWENDOLYN. *(to catch* **MEREDITH***'s attention)* Psssstt!

(**MEREDITH** *truns and is surprised to see her ghostly friends.*)

MEREDITH. What are you guys doing here?

LILLIPUT. We've come to say…

ALL. "GOOD JOB"

(**PATTY** *and* **PATRICK** *strike a cheerleader pose.*)

GWENDOLYN. We saw the whole thing.

(indicating to the ceiling)

From "up there."

LILLIPUT. Great speech at the end!

MEREDITH. Thanks. But I should thank you. I couldn't have done it without you.

PATTY & PATRICK. *(as a cheer with a pose at the end)* THHHHAAAAAAAAAAAAAAAAATTTTTTTTT'S RIGHT!

LILLIPUT. You were quite a project!

GWENDOLYN. BUT, well worth it!

MEREDITH. I'm sure I seemed impossible.

GWENDOLYN. But we make the impossible, possible.

LILLIPUT. It's our specialty!

PATTY & PATRICK. *(as a cheer with a pose at the end)* THHHHAAAAAAAAAAAAAAAAAAATTTTTTTTTTTTT'S RIGHT!

MEREDITH. You worked a miracle.

GWENDOLYN. Our pleasure.

MEREDITH. I gotta go…

LILLIPUT. We know. You've got a show.

GWENDOLYN. Do you mind if we hang around and watch the play? I love Shakespeare.

LILLIPUT. Shakespeare and I briefly dated in college.

MEREDITH. I don't think we have any seats left.

GWENDOLYN. Seats?! We don't need seats! We'll just hover in the rafters.

MEREDITH. Well, sure then. I'd love for you to see it. Melissa is going to be *fantastic*!

LILLIPUT. You're turning out to be pretty fantastic yourself.

MEREDITH. Thanks to you guys.

MS. CHENAULT. *(from the back of the house)* PLACES FOR ACT ONE!

MEREDITH. I gotta go! Oh, I'm *so* excited!

GWENDOLYN. GO!

*(**MEREDITH** starts out.)*

Oh…

*(**MEREDITH** stops.)*

FYI, Casper and I are history. I'm dating this big lug now.

*(She indicates **FUTURE**.)*

I love the strong and silent type.

(beat)

GO!

PATTY & PATRICK. *(as a cheer)* BREAK. A. LEG.

(And they pose.)

*(**MEREDITH** runs off. **GWENDOLYN** faces the others.)*

GWENDOLYN. Ok, kids – back to the rafters.

(They ad lib as they exit. From the house we hear…)

MS. CHENAULT. ANNNNNDDDDD…LIGHTS

(There is an immediate blackout and Medieval music explodes through the speakers.)

The End

APPENDIX
Optional Scene

The following scene replaces the middle of Scene Five in the event the producing company opts for not using small children characters:

MELVIN. *(still imitating)* "My daddy has a plane! My mother has a yacht! My parents are wherever I am not!"

(Everyone continues laughing.)

LYDIA. That was great, Melvin!

SERENA. Absolutely perfect!

TIFFANY. Fits Meredith like a cashmere sweater!

MELVIN. *(in a British accent)* Why thank you, kind ladies. Thank you very much!

MONTY. Yeah. Melvin's a regular ole Shakespeare.

BILLY. DON'T mention the word "Shakespeare" around me, please. I'm really, really, really nervous about *Romeo and Juliet.*

SERENA. Why are you nervous, Billy. You know your lines.

BILLY. Yeah. I do, but Meredith doesn't!

TIFFANY. OH! That reminds me. I nearly forgot! I've got some juicy gossip about Meredith to tell you guys!

MONTY. What?

MELVIN. It's not nice to gossip.

TIFFANY. Well, Meredith's not nice. So any gossip about her is fair game and deserved.

(beat)

Wanna know what it is?

LYDIA. Tiffany, what are you talking about?

TIFFANY. You know. That juicy little bit of news Melissa told us at cheerleading practice!

SERENA. Tiffany, you *can't* tell that. We *promised!*

LYDIA. Yeah – we gave the green and white promise!

MELVIN. What's the green and white promise?

TIFFANY. It's a cheerleader thing. You wouldn't understand.

MELVIN. Okay.

MONTY. So. What is it?

TIFFANY. Okay. Well…Melissa told us…

LYDIA. If Meredith finds out you told, she's gonna kill you.

TIFFANY. So what.

> *(beat)*

> Anyway, Ms. Chenault called Mellisa and asked her to be Juliet.

BILLY. You mean instead of Meredith?

TIFFANY. Yes. Instead of Meredith.

> *(There is a pause.)*

MONTY. That. Is. So. COOL!

BILLY. My opinion of Ms. Cheault just shot up two kajillion points!

MELVIN. This is going to be the best play, ever!

BILLY. This is going to be the best Christmas ever!

MONTY. THANK YOU SANTA CLAUS!

LYDIA. Wait. Don't get too excited. Melissa isn't going to take the part.

BILLY. Why not! She *has* too!

MELVIN. If she doesn't, the play is going to be stinky. Putrid. Gross. Eck. Ewww. Icky. Blechhh!

TIFFANY. Melvin. We got it.

SERENA. Melissa doesn't want to be Juliet because she doesn't want to hurt Meredith's feelings.

BILLY. Ok. Number one, Meredith doesn't *have* feelings.

MONTY. Yeah. Remember what she did to Melissa at the dance last year?

MELVIN. Yeah. That was really most uncool.

SERENA. Meredith is Melissa's best friend.

BILLY. *(laughing)* Her *best* friend? How can Melissa say that with the way Meredith treats her?

MONTY. Yeah. Meredith's best friend is Meredith. In fact, Meredith's *only* friend is Meredith.

MELVIN. As much as I dislike Meredith, I respect Melissa's loyalty. But I hope she double crosses Meredith and takes the part. That would be just the kick in the teeth Meredith deserves.

LYDIA. Okay, okay, okay...enough talk about Meredith! It's Christmas! Let's not ruin it thinking about her. We have a PARTY to get ready for!

TIFFANY. I am so excited!

MONTY. When are the elementary kids supposed to get here?

TIFFANY. Any moment. Okay. I've planned all kinds of fun things for us to do. We're going to PLAY GAMES!

(Everyone is silent.)

Guys. You're supposed to yell enthusiastically after I say PLAY GAMES!

EVERYONE. Oh. Okay. Sorry. "YAY!"

TIFFANY. And HAVE SNACKS!

EVERYONE. YAY!

TIFFANY. SING CAROLS!

EVERYONE. YAY!

TIFFANY. And have TONS OF FUN!

EVERYONE. YAY!

TIFFANY. SO ARE YOU GUYS READY?!?

EVERYONE. YES!

TIFFANY. I SAID ARE YOU GUYS READY?!?

EVERYONE. YES!!!

TIFFANY. THEN LET'S GO OUT THERE AND SHOW THOSE KIDS A GREAT TIME!

EVERYONE. YAY!

(General ad libs of enthusiasm as everyone exits, including **MEREDITH** *who begins to exit with the group.* **LILLIPUT** *stops her.)*

The script picks up with LILLIPUT'S line: "Where do you think you're going?"

Also by
Mark Landon Smith...

**A Dickens Christmas Carol:
A Travelling Travesty in Two
Tumultuous Acts**

Dupont, Mississippi

Faith County

**Faith County II:
An Evening of Culture**

Hindenberg!

The Pirate Show

Radio T.B.S.

**The Really Hip Adventures
of Go-Go Girl**

Please visit our website **bakersplays.com** for complete
descriptions and licensing information.

OTHER TITLES AVAILABLE FROM BAKER'S PLAYS

THE REALLY HIP ADVENTURES OF GO-GO GIRL

Mark Landon Smith

YTA, Children's Theatre / 11f / 4m / Multiple Sets, simply suggested

The Really Hip Adventures of Go-Go Girl - Episode 9:
Space Vixens with Sassy Attitudes

From the author of the sensational hit comedy *Faith County* comes a cosmic take-off on the low budget science-fiction/teen beach movies of the '50s and '60s. Four beauty pageant contestants, en route to the Miss Magic Oval Lift Panty Pageant, are captured in the tail of a passing comet, and hurtled to the planet of Sniggle O' Cheese. Nanette and Phoebe are treated as goddesses, while Mavis and Oma — victims of "Bouffant Fusion" during the crash — are sent back to Earth with Asian guide Moo Goo Gai Pan to steal Mystery Formula X, a substance vital to the planet's existence! It's up to Go-Go Girl — cleverly disguised as Babs Broadway, popular coed at Nancy Sinatra State University — to defend her planet from the extraterrestrials. With the help of her friends, she begins an adventure of interplanetary proportions! An action-packed romp through every B-movie cliche.